Helen Gustafson

Dinner's Ready Mom

with Illustrations by Jill Gustafson

CELESTIALARTS

Berkeley, California

Celestial Arts
P.O. Box 7327
Berkeley, California 94707

First Printing, 1986

Cover and interior book design by Ken Scott
Typography by Ann Flanagan Typography

Library of Congress Cataloging-in-Publication Data

Gustafson, Helen.
  Dinner's Ready Mom.
  Includes index.
  Summary: Offers simple menus and step-by-step instructions for a variety of dinner dishes that may be prepared by children alone. Also discusses basic cooking techniques and equipment.
  1. Cookery—Juvenile literature. [1. Cookery]
I. Title.
TX652.5G86 1986   641.5′123   86-11802
ISBN 0-89087-470-0

Manufactured in the United States of America
            89 90 — 0 9 8 7 6 5 4 3

Acknowledgments

Celestial Arts editor, David Hinds, with his usual generosity, tells me I may thank everybody. Here goes:

For son Paul Gustafson, my inventive and steady cook, my first thank you.

For daughter Jill who illustrated the text and for Gus who coached us all, my sweet thanks.

For Patricia Curtan, who edited the text and consulted on the menus, a bouquet of thanks.

Big thanks to friends, neighbors, and testers: next door Lynne Cahoon and daughter Cheryl, Mijo and Sarah Horwich, Ellie and Grace Gilbert. Advisors Teresa Chris, Brad Bunnin, Joan Finton, and Sabina Johnson. Proofreaders Dr. F. M. Epstein and Jill Graham.

Thanks to Sandra Wooten, Barbara Wolfinger, Vern Sutcher, Sahag Avedisian, Joy Carlin, Barbara Hodovan, Patty Peterson, Audrey and Phil Elwood, Swati and Andy and Ritu Mukerji, Franz Snyder, Trish Hawthorne, Sally Little, Dr. Robert Moulton, Barbara Costa and Janet Snidow, Kieron Edwards, Jessica Lee, Chris Flanagan, and Linda Harris.

Special thanks to Judith Steinhart and to my research committee in the Southland: Joan and Bertha Gustafson and Lois Flanagan.

Special thanks to the first school to take the plunge, Cornell School in Albany, California: principal Bob Alpert and secretary Helen Walker; teachers Linda Nielsen, Lucy Hamai, Sara Danielson, Hanae Nishioka, Shirley McGinnis, Tom Gamba, and Susan Butch; and students Tina Clark, Bobby Blank, Himanshu Koirala, Kelly Mirabella, Muaz Nuruddin, Brian Manning, Timbu Massango, Rita Willis, Mark Choi, Hadiyah Abdul-Mumin, Kate Clancy, Cuong Quach, and April Singer. At the School of the Madeleine, principal Sister Mary Allyn, O.P.; Sister Mary Louise; and students Andre Fedan, Charisma Baltadano, Matt Whelan, Julie Martinez, Pat Harvey, Gabrielle Flavin, Simon Burcham, Trevor Stearns, Kathryn Karst, Randall Doran, Tristine Glick, Karen Webster, Andrea Balazs, and Tom O'Neill.

For his unflagging coaching on textual matters, my gratitude to Fritz Streiff.

For the laying on of hands and early inspiration, Marion Cunningham, Ellen Siegelman, and my first friend in Berkeley, Mary Goldstein.

Please Read!!!

Not even a carefully written book can substitute for parental guidance and supervision, and this book is no exception. Be sure your child understands that the kitchen and its contents must be treated with respect and care: knives can cut and stoves can burn. Be sure you've satisfied yourself that your child can work safely in your kitchen—although you're not watching and helping before trusting him or her to work alone.

C O N T E N T S

Chicken

Eggs & Cheese

Beef

Fish

Lamb, Ham, Pork, & Sausages

Desserts

Garlic Bread

*Experienced cooks <u>only</u>!

Mom's Pork Chops

Baked pork chops with a rich tomato sauce— sister dish to the lamb chops.

Start to finish: 2 hours

THIS IS HOW YOUR BOOK SHOULD LOOK!

P.S.
This is a real
recipe

Needed:

Adjust quantity to suit your family.

4 large baking potatoes

4 to 6 loin or center cut pork chops, ½ inch to ¾ inch thick

1 red onion *or white*

1 can Campbell's chicken gumbo soup

1 small can stewed tomatoes (8 ounces)

Raw vegetables for salad: green pepper, cucumber, celery, etc., or salad greens and dressing

10- or 12-inch oven-proof frying pan

hange times to fit
our dinner time.

4:30 Turn the oven on to 350°.

Scrub and cut the ends off 4 baking potatoes and put them in the oven right on the rack.

5:30 Put the pork chops in a big 10- or 12-inch oven-proof frying pan [*big black one*].

Cut the onion in rings and put some on each pork chop.

Pour the can of soup and stewed tomatoes over all, and put the frying pan in the oven, uncovered.

6:15 Cut up some raw vegetables such as green pepper, celery, cucumber, etc., and put on a plate for a salad, or make a leafy green salad (see inside cover pages).

6:25 Set the table.

6:30 Serve the chops on plates with some sauce from the pan—don't forget the potatoes and salad—and...EAT!

*Remember to use
the right pans!*

Your notes

Dad's favorite
Chops can be fried _then_ put in
the big blue roasting pan.
OK with canned or fresh tomatoes

**The empty brackets are for you to write in
the best pot or pan your Mom wants you to use.**

Chicken

Lemon Dagger Chicken

A roasted chicken favorite with delicious potatoes.

Start to finish: 1 hour 30 minutes

Needed:

3 to 4 pound whole chicken

2 lemons

2 or 3 large baking potatoes

Salad greens and dressing

Canned or bottled applesauce, medium size

Salt

Pepper

9 × 13-inch cake pan

Apple slicer

Kitchen scissors

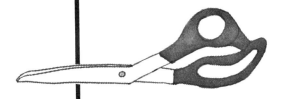

5:00 Turn the oven on to 350°.

Take the bag of parts out of the chicken. Drain any liquid that may be inside.

Cut off the little tail at the bottom opening and the fatty parts with a kitchen scissors.

Sprinkle about 1/4 teaspoon salt and 1/4 teaspoon pepper all over the outside of the chicken and rub a little inside, too.

Now the dagger part: Rinse the 2 lemons and puncture them 15 to 20 times with a fork or shishkebab skewer. Put the lemons inside the chicken (so that one is in front of the other).

5:15 Put the chicken on its back in a 9×13 inch cake pan [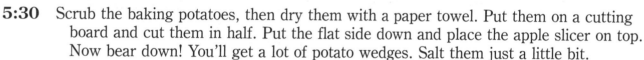] and put it in the oven uncovered.

5:30 Scrub the baking potatoes, then dry them with a paper towel. Put them on a cutting board and cut them in half. Put the flat side down and place the apple slicer on top. Now bear down! You'll get a lot of potato wedges. Salt them just a little bit.

Take the chicken pan out of the oven, put all the potato slices around the chicken, and put the chicken back in.

6:00 Turn the oven up to 400°.

6:05 Set the table and make a green salad. (See inside cover pages.)

6:25 Get Mom or Dad to carve the chicken—it's messy! Put a bowl of applesauce on the table with a serving spoon.

6:30 Serve the chicken with the roast potatoes and EAT!

Chinese Chicken

A real stand-by—crispy baked chicken with fluffy white rice.

Start to finish: 1 hour 15 minutes

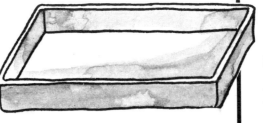

Needed:

10 to 12 chicken pieces—
wings and legs are best

¼ cup soy sauce, or "lite"
soy sauce (which is less
salty)

1 teaspoon curry powder

¼ cup orange juice

¼ cup dry sherry, or
¼ cup pear juice from
canned pears

1 cup rice

Pear salad:
Lettuce leaves
1 16-ounce can pear halves
About 3 to 4 ounces
cheddar cheese
Walnuts

9×13-inch cake pan

Large kitchen fork

5:15 Turn the oven on to 425°.

Put the chicken pieces in a 9-inch by 13-inch cake pan [   ].

Mix together in a bowl, soy sauce, orange juice, dry sherry or pear juice, and curry powder.

5:30 Pour this mixture over the chicken pieces and put the pan in the oven.

5:45 Turn the oven down to 350° and, with a large kitchen fork, turn over the chicken pieces.

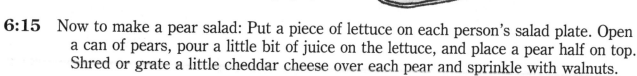

6:00 Set the table.

6:05 Start the rice (see inside cover pages).

6:15 Now to make a pear salad: Put a piece of lettuce on each person's salad plate. Open a can of pears, pour a little bit of juice on the lettuce, and place a pear half on top. Shred or grate a little cheddar cheese over each pear and sprinkle with walnuts.

6:30 Serve the chicken and sauce next to the rice, put the salad plates on the side, and...EAT!

Ugly-but-good Chicken

Chicken roasted upside down with onions and potatoes. That's it—ugly, but good.

Start to finish: 1 hour 45 minutes

Needed:

3 to 4 pound whole chicken

4 yellow onions

4 medium size, any kind potatoes

1 Stouffer's spinach souffle for 4

Radishes and celery for salad

Salt

Cookie sheet with sides (15 × 10½ inches, or even larger)

Large kitchen fork

4:45   Turn the oven on to 375°.

Dry the chicken with a paper towel and pat on *2 tablespoons* ordinary table salt all over the skin—not any inside, please!

Put it breast-side down on a large cookie sheet with sides.

Cut the yellow onions in half and put around the chicken.

Wash the potatoes, cut them in half, and put face down on the cookie sheet around the chicken. Put the cookie sheet in the oven.

Take the cover off the souffle and put it on the middle rack of the oven.

6:10   Prepare a tray of radishes and celery sticks and set the table.

6:20   Use oven mitts and remove the cookie sheet from the oven and take it over to the sink. Then spear the chicken through the neck opening with a large fork so you can pick it up safely. Now hold the chicken over the sink and use your other hand to whack off the crusty salt with a wooden spoon. Then put the chicken back on the cookie sheet and tear off the skin. Toss the chicken skin in the sink—you can clean up later.

Baking the chicken with this heavy crust of salt makes it very moist and tasty, but this much salt needs to be removed before eating the meat. Hang in there—this one is really worth all the effort!

6:30   Put a serving of chicken, onions, potatoes, and souffle on each plate and…EAT!

Cheryl's Chicken Casserole

A casserole dish—crispy and gooey at the same time.

Start to finish: 1 hour 50 minutes

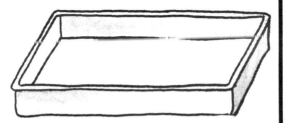

Needed:

½ package Knorr's*
dry onion soup mix
(approximately)

1 cup white rice

Salt

Pepper

10¾-ounce can Campbell's
cream of chicken soup

1 teaspoon fresh or dried
rosemary

½ cup Parmesan cheese

6 to 8 chicken pieces

Salad of your choice

French bread

9×13-inch cake pan

*Lipton's is a second choice

4:40 Turn the oven on to 325°.

Spread half a package onion soup mix on the bottom of a 9 × 13-inch cake pan [   ].

Pour the uncooked rice over the soup mix.

Open the can of soup and spread it as evenly as you can over the rice.

Fill the can with water and pour that over too.

Sprinkle about 1 teaspoon fresh or dried rosemary over the soup, then add about 1/2 cup Parmesan cheese over all.

Last put the chicken pieces on top, skin side up, and season with a pinch salt and pepper.

5:00 Put the pan in the oven uncovered. Take a break now, and then at...

6:10 Make a salad of your choice (see inside cover pages).

6:20 Set the table, put the French bread and butter on, serve the chicken and rice and...EAT!

Garbanzo Chicken Stew

A delicious saucy chicken stew— good enough for guests.

Start to finish: 2 hours 15 minutes

Needed:

6 to 8 pieces chicken

8 boiling onions

2 cloves garlic (cut in halves)

Salt

1 can pear halves (or pieces) 16 oz.

1 can, about 15 ounces, garbanzo beans

8-ounce package Jiffy Corn Muffin Mix
Requires:
   1 egg
   ⅓ cup milk

Salad greens and dressing

Deep, heavy pot with a lid

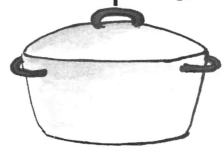

4:15 Put the chicken pieces in a deep heavy pot with a lid [   ].

Then put in 8 unpeeled boiling onions. (You *may* peel if you wish!)

Next, sprinkle about 1/4 teaspoon salt over the onions and chicken and add the garlic cloves, cut into halves.

Add the pear juice. Save the pears and chill them to eat for dessert.*

Open the can of beans and pour them in the pot, juice and all.

4:30 Put the lid on the pot and place on top of the stove over low heat. It should simmer gently—just barely bubbling.

5:50 Turn the oven on to 400°, and mix the cornbread according to the directions on the packages. Let it sit in the pan a moment or two.

6:00 Put the cornbread in the oven. Take the lid off the chicken pot.

6:05 Make a green salad.

6:15 Set the table.

6:30 Put the bowl of greens and a salad dressing on the table so that each person can make an individual salad. Put the cornbread on a hot pad on the table. Serve everyone a plate with some of the chicken, onions, beans and...EAT!

*Serve with ice cream and walnuts and/or chocolate sauce if you have it in the house.

Franz's Chicken Paprika Stew

A chicken stew with gorgeous pink sauce.

Start to finish: 1 hour 30 minutes

Needed:

1 to 2 tablespoons butter

3 yellow onions

6 to 8 chicken pieces

2 10¾-ounce cans Campbell's chicken broth

2 tablespoons paprika (Hungarian is best, but because it's delicate, 2 tablespoons are needed.)

or:

2 teaspoons regular paprika

Fresh vegetables for salad: carrots, celery, turnips, etc.

Half of an 8-ounce carton of sour cream

3 slices of Northridge or Pepperidge Farm white bread

Deep, heavy pot with a lid

5:00 In a deep heavy pot with a lid put a hunk of butter as big as a walnut
[   ].

Peel and slice 3 onions and add to the pot. Cook on low heat until the onions are a pretty golden yellow color—but *not browned!*

Place the chicken pieces in the pot.

Pour the cans of clear chicken broth over the chicken and mix in 2 tablespoons Hungarian paprika (or 2 teaspoons regular paprika).

Put the cover on and turn the heat up to medium. It should gently simmer—just barely bubbling.

6:20 Cut up fresh vegetables for salad: carrots, celery, turnips, etc., and put them on a big dinner plate for nibbling.

6:25 Add 6 to 8 tablespoons of sour cream to the sides of the pot—but don't stir it. You will get a pretty pink marbleized effect this way.

6:28 Toast the bread and cut it in triangles.

6:30 Ladle the chicken into soup bowls or deep dinner plates and arrange the toast triangles on the side, ready to sop up the sauce and…EAT!

Harriet's Home Chicken-in-a Pot

A classic, easy chicken-in-a-pot dish—known to cure the blues.

This is a simple, comforting dinner for a family member or friend who doesn't feel well. (For a simpler version, cook it without the vegetables.)

Start to finish: 1 hour 45 minutes

Needed:

1 whole 3 to 4 pound chicken

2 tablespoons butter

½ teaspoon basil

¼ teaspoon oregano

Salt

Pepper

2 cloves garlic (whole or halved)

If you wish:

6 large carrots

3 medium-size red potatoes

1 lemon

1 medium-size jar applesauce

1 loaf egg bread (chala or other)

Deep, heavy pan with a lid

Large kitchen fork

Kitchen scissors

4:45 Turn the oven on to 350°.

Take the parts out of the chicken, place in a plastic bag, and freeze for later. With a kitchen scissors trim away some of the fat near the bottom opening.

Put a blob of butter as big as a walnut in a heavy oven-proof, deep-sided pot with a lid [   ]. (Keep the lid off till 5:15.)

Put the pot on a burner over medium-high heat. Place the chicken in it and let the chicken brown on one side (5 minutes or so).

Turn the chicken over and brown the other side.

Use the large kitchen fork to set the chicken on its back; then sprinkle on about 1/2 teaspoon salt, 1/2 teaspoon pepper, 1/4 teaspoon basil, 1/4 teaspoon oregano, and 2 cloves garlic (whole or halved). Let the chicken continue cooking while you prepare the vegetables.

Pare the carrots, slice them at an angle, and add to the pot.

Scrub the potatoes, cut them into large chunks, unpeeled, and add to the pot as well.

5:15 Put the cover on the pot and put it in the oven.

6:30 Using oven mitts, remove the pot from the oven. Remove the lid and, with the large kitchen fork, lift out the chicken. Squeeze a lemon over it. Get some help carving it and serve it with the vegetables. Don't forget the applesauce and bread, and—yes—EAT!

Mom's Lemon Chicken & Rice Casserole

A good casserole dish—travels well—kids love it.

Start to finish: 2 hours

Needed:

1½ teaspoons pureed bottled garlic or 4 to 5 cloves freshly pressed garlic (to make 1½ teaspoons)

1 cup white rice

8 chicken pieces

1 14¼-ounce can Swanson's clear chicken broth

2 lemons

Salad greens and dressing

Loaf fresh bread

9×13-inch cake pan

4:30   Turn on the oven to 350°.

Spread or dot 1-1/2 teaspoons freshly pressed garlic or 1-1/2 teaspoons pureed bottled garlic all over the bottom of a 9×13-inch cake pan.

Pour the uncooked rice evenly over the garlic.

Put the chicken pieces on top of the rice, evenly spaced in the pan.

Sprinkle about 1/4 teaspoon salt and 1/4 teaspoon pepper over the chicken.

Open the can of clear chicken broth and pour over everything.

Cut each lemon into 4 slices and put one slice on top of each piece of chicken; then cover the pan tightly with foil.

5:00   Put the pan in the oven.

6:15   Make a green salad with your choice of dressing (see inside cover pages).

6:25   Set the table and put the bread on now.

6:30   Use a big spatula or spoon to serve the chicken and rice onto dinner plates. Put the salad on the table and...EAT!

For a crispier dish, take the foil off (with help) at 6:15.

Patricia Edwards' Honey-butter Chicken

(& Sunny Squash Casserole)

*Roasted luxury chicken—
good enough for guests,
but simple to prepare.*

Start to finish: 1 hour 40 minutes

*To soften butter, place the
butter (in its paper) on the
counter and press down!

Needed:

¼ cup honey

½ cup (1 stick) butter

3 to 4 pound whole chicken

4 zucchini squash

4 yellow crookneck squash
   or similar types of squash

Salt, Pepper

2 yellow onions

½ teaspoon pureed bottled
   garlic or 1 to 2 cloves
   fresh garlic to make ½
   teaspoon

8-ounce package Jiffy Corn
   Muffin Mix—Requires:
   1 egg
   ⅓ cup milk
   8-inch pie or cake pan

Fresh raw vegetables for
   salad

9 × 13-inch cake pan   Kitchen scisso

4:50   Turn the oven on to 425°.

Mix together 1/4 cup honey and 1/4 cup (half a stick) soft butter in a small bowl.

With a kitchen scissors cut off the little tail and fatty parts at the bottom opening.

Take the parts out of the chicken and freeze for later use.

Smear the honey-butter mixture all over the outside of the chicken.

Put the chicken on its back in a 9 × 13-inch cake pan [   ] and put it in the oven uncovered.

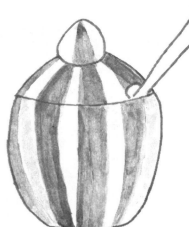

5:05   Wash the different squashes, then cut across in slices about as wide as your finger. You should have a total of about 4 to 5 cups of squash.

Lay them in another 9 × 13-inch cake pan [   ].

Cut 2 yellow onions into quarters and mix them in with the squash.

Slice the remaining half of the butter into 4 thin slices and space them out across the pan.

Dot the top of the squash with 4 tiny spoonfuls of pureed bottled garlic (about 1/2 teaspoon in all) or 1 to 2 cloves freshly pressed garlic to make 1/2 teaspoon.

Sprinkle on about 1/4 teaspoon salt and 1/2 teaspoon pepper. Give the whole thing a stir and cover the pan with foil.

5:25   Put the squash pan in the oven and turn the heat down to 350°.

5:50   Make the cornbread according to the directions on the package. Bake it in an 8-inch pie or cake pan.

6:00   Turn the oven up to 400° and put the cornbread in. Yes, there are three things in the oven at once.

6:15   Set the table. Cut some celery, tomatoes, cucumbers, whatever fresh vegetables you have to make a salad.

6:25   Put the cornbread on the table with a hot pad underneath it.

Get Mom or Dad to help you carve the chicken.

6:30   Serve the squash and chicken on to plates and...EAT!

Sarah's
Russian Rosemary
Fried Chicken

*Fried chicken and shoestring potatoes
—an excellent and quick dinner.*

Start to finish: 1 hour

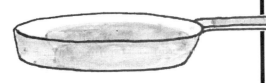

Needed:

6 chicken thighs (or breasts cut into quarters)

3 tablespoons olive oil or vegetable oil

Salt

6 sprigs fresh rosemary or 2 teaspoons dried rosemary

3 large baking (russet) potatoes

Green salad or raw vegetables for salad

Heavy, 12-inch frying pan—cast iron is best

Vegetable grater

5:30 Salt the skin side of the chicken thighs or pieces with about 1 teaspoon salt.

Pour 3 tablespoons olive oil or vegetable oil into a big heavy 12-inch frying pan with a lid [   ].

5:40 Put the pan on the stove over medium-high heat and when the oil bubbles a little bit, about 3 minutes, place the chicken pieces in the pan, skin side down. Put a sprig of rosemary or pinch of dried rosemary on top of each piece of chicken, and while it begins to brown, start to prepare the potatoes.

5:50 Wipe the potatoes clean with a damp paper towel. Don't peel them. Shred them all on a grater on the side with the largest holes. They will look like hashbrowns.

Spread them out on paper towels and blot *dry* with more paper towels.

6:00 Tuck the potatoes around the chicken pieces. It will look quite pretty—the green rosemary, the pink chicken, and the white shredded potatoes. Put the lid on and turn the heat down to medium-low. Cook it that way till time to serve, about 30 minutes.

6:10 Set the table. Made a green salad with your choice of dressing (see inside cover pages), or prepare a plate of cut-up raw vegetables.

6:25 Take the cover off and look at the chicken and potatoes. When they are brown around the edges, take a big spatula and serve on to dinner plates.

6:30 EAT!

Good show! A little tricky this dinner, but good.

P.S. You can substitute any herb that the family likes for the rosemary.

Eggs & Cheese

Macaroni & Cheese

The simplest version ever.

Start to finish: 20 minutes

Needed:

8 ounces elbow macaroni

or

6 ounces egg noodles

4 to 6 ounces cheddar cheese or your favorite cheese (about half a bar)

Salt

Fresh veggies for munching: cucumbers, green peppers, celery, carrots, cherry tomatoes, etc.

No times given here—eat it whenever you like!

Fill a 2-quart sauce pan [   ] three-quarters full with cold water.

Add 1/2 teaspoon salt to the water.

Put it on a burner over high heat.

When it boils, add the macaroni or noodles.

Turn down the heat to medium and boil for 8 to 12 minutes. DO NOT COVER!

Shred about 1-1/2 cups of cheese onto a small plate.

After 8 minutes or so of cooking, test the macaroni for doneness. Lift some out with a slotted spoon, let it cool for a moment or two, and taste. If macaroni is soft and tender, it's done. If not soft, cook for 2 to 3 minutes longer.

Put a drainer in the sink and pour the water and noodles into it.

Hold the pot handle with respect—that water is *HOT.*

Now dump the drained noodles right back into the hot pan, throw the cheese in, give it a stir, and put a lid on it.

Make yourself wait for five minutes before you serve to let the cheese melt, then…EAT!

Be sure to eat the veggies too—good for you!

Supervision Sandwiches

Big melted cheese, tomato and green pepper super sandwich ...can be a meal.

Start to finish: about 45 minutes

Needed:

8 slices whole wheat bread

2 large ripe tomatoes

1 green pepper

¾ to 1 pound aged cheddar cheese

A selection of fresh fruit: apples, bananas, oranges, grapes, etc.

Large bag corn chips

If you wish—
    8 slices bacon
    pickle slices

These are yummy. After you build them, wait for a parent to supervise the actual broiling of the sandwiches.

6:00   Lightly toast the whole-wheat bread. Lay the pieces out on a large cutting board and begin to build the sandwiches. Cut the tomatoes into slices about 1/4 inch thick and put one on each piece of bread.

Cut the green pepper into little wedges about as wide as your finger and put 2 or 3 on top of the tomato.

Slice the cheese and lay several slices on each sandwich so that the tomato and green peppers are covered.

6:20   Set the table. Put the fruit and corn chips in bowls and put on the table.

6:25   Now get some supervision for broiling the sandwiches. They should be on the middle rack of the broiler, about 2 inches from the heat. Broil until the cheese is just melted and lightly browned.

6:30   Serve nice and hot and...EAT!

For a spicy note, add little pickle slices to the sandwiches. To be really wicked, fry 8 pieces bacon before starting, dry, and place on top of the melted cheese as a garnish. Sparkling apple cider and popcorn also are a lovely addition.

These sandwiches are our Christmas Eve ritual—served picnic style in front of the fireplace.

Bob's Emergency Cheese Dish

Anytime when the cupboard is bare and all you have in the house is some stale bread, a bit of milk, and odds and ends of old cheese, you can make an Emergency Supper.

Start to finish: about 50 minutes

Needed:

2 eggs

About 2 to 2½ cups milk

Old bread pieces—crusty and soft

2 or 3 kinds cheese, about 1 cup

cheddar, jack, Swiss, Parmesan, etc.

1 to 2 teaspoons mustard

7×4-inch bread pan

Serve with cottage cheese and celery if you have it

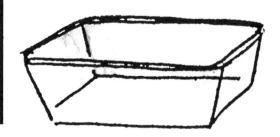

5:40 Turn the oven on to 350°.

With a fork beat up 2 eggs in an ordinary-size bread pan, 7-inches by 4-inches.

Then fill it half-full with milk (about 2 to 2 1/2 cups), low-fat milk is O.K.

Tear bread pieces, crusty and soft, into hunks about as big as your thumb.

Put enough bread in the pan so it's comfortably full—*not* jammed full.

Put 10 to 15 little chunks of cheese (roughly 1 cup) all around the bread. Any mixture will do: cheddar, jack, Swiss, Parmesan—at least 2 or 3 kinds, the more variety the better.

Dab about 6 dots of mustard, in drops about as big as a penny, over the top.

6:00 Bake uncovered for *about* half an hour or *until golden brown*. The look of it is more important than the actual time.

6:30 EAT! This is like a souffle. It will be light, melting and soft, and yummy! Even though the supper is made with cheese, it goes very well with cold cottage cheese and celery.

Quick-Mex Supper

A baked egg and chili casserole—has the flavor of chili rellenos. Madly popular—this is one version out of many.

Start to finish: 1 hour 20 minutes

If packaged shredded cheeses are not available, cut a bar of cheese in half and use your grater!

Exact ounces don't matter.

The different kinds of cheeses make this dish interesting, but the exact quantities of each kind really don't matter.

Needed:

4 eggs

4-ounce package sliced jack cheese

4-ounce package shredded cheddar cheese

4-ounce can Ortega whole green chilis, contains 4 chilis—not chili peppers!

¼ cup mild taco sauce, green or red

4-ounce package shredded mozzarella cheese

1 package corn tortillas

3 or 4 tomatoes and dressing

If you wish: small (8 ounce) carton sour cream

8×8-inch cake pan

5:10 Turn the oven on to 325°.

Beat 4 eggs in the bottom of an 8-inch by 8-inch cake pan (pyrex or metal are both O.K.), until foamy. No need to grease the pan.

Place the pieces of jack cheese all over the bottom of the cake pan on top of the beaten eggs.

Then sprinkle the shredded cheddar cheese on top of that.

Place the 4 chilis on top of the cheeses and spread them over the whole pan.

Dot the top of each chili with a little taco sauce—no more than 1/4 cup total.

Top off with mozzarella cheese on the chilis.

5:40 Put the pan in the oven uncovered.

5:45 Take the tortillas out of the package and wrap them in foil, making a tight packet. Put them in the oven to warm.

5:50 Set the table.

6:00 Wash and slice the tomatoes, arrange on a dish, and pour over some dressing (see inside cover pages).

6:25 Take the pan out of the oven and cut big squares with a spatula and serve directly on to dinner plates. Put on the table with the tortillas and tomato salad and…

6:30 EAT!

Dinner Dutch Bunny

*An egg and meat dish—
like quiche without a crust.*

*This makes a very light little
supper dish or a substantial contribution to breakfast.*

*For a "Just We Two" dinner,
divide every ingredient in half. So for this recipe it
would be 2 tablespoons butter, 2 large eggs, etc.
Use as much salami or ham as you wish.
But, be sure to use only an 8-inch frying pan
or cake pan!*

Start to finish: 30 minutes

Needed:

4 tablespoons butter or
   margarine

4 large eggs, or 5 small ones

1 cup milk

1 cup all-purpose flour

About 2 cups total of any
   of the following: salami,
   cooked or left over
   sausages or ham, cheese,
   green pepper, celery,
   or other veggies. Any
   combination of these is
   very tasty, especially
   salami and cheese.

9 × 13-inch cake pan

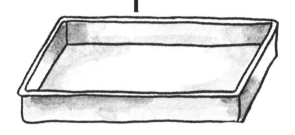

6:00   Turn the oven on to 425°.

Put 2 blobs of butter or margarine (about 2 tablespoons) into a 9 × 13 inch cake pan
    [   ], and put the pan in the oven.

In a mixing bowl, beat the eggs, until bubbles appear, then add the milk, then add the
    flour. It will be a little lumpy—that's OK.

6:15   With an oven mitt or pot holders take the pan out of the oven and pour in the egg
    mixture. Then put the pan back in the oven.

Now chop the salami, sausages, cheeses, or whatever into small pieces.

6:20   Use an oven mitt and take the pan out of the oven again. Drop in the pieces of
    meat, etc. If you are using cheese, add that last. Return it to the oven once more.

6:30   It's done! Take the pan out, cut up the Dutch Bunny with a spatula into big wedges
    and put on dinner plates, and...EAT! right now!

Beef

Cedar Grove Parkway Stew

Beef stew, very popular and easy—no browning of the meat.

Start to finish: 2 hours 30 minutes

Needed:

2 pounds cut-up beef stew meat

12 boiling onions* (or 4 yellow onions each cut into four pieces)

6 carrots

24 ounces V-8 juice

¼ cup quick-cooking minute tapioca

Salad greens and dressing

French bread or other fresh bread

Deep, heavy pot with a lid

Vegetable peeler

Boiling onions are white—and about as big as a walnut.

4:00 Turn the oven on to 350°.

Put the stew meat into a deep heavy pot with a lid. [   ]

Add the boiling onions, unpeeled...or peel, if you like.

Peel the carrots with a vegetable peeler, cut in slices, and add to the pot.

Pour in the V-8 juice.

Season with 1/4 teaspoon each salt and pepper, and add 1/4 cup uncooked tapioca.

(No potatoes, please! They will turn to mush.)

about
4:20 Put the lid on the pot and put it in the oven.

6:10 Make a green salad with the dressing of your choice (see inside cover pages).

6:20 Set the table and put a loaf of French bread in the oven.

6:30 Serve the stew with some warm crusty French bread and salad, and...EAT!

Spaghetti "Dish"

Dinner in a dish—browned meat and spaghetti and tomato sauce. Gooey and slurpy, like spaghetti.

Dish "Deluxe": Add a thinly sliced carrot along with the green pepper. This is the recipe that started it all! It was created by my grandma, who loved "one-dish dishes."

Start to finish: 1 hour

Needed:

1 large yellow onion

1 pound lean ground round hamburger meat

Salt

Pepper

2 cloves garlic

1 large green pepper

10¾-ounce can Campbell's Tomato Bisque soup

About 1/8 pound spaghetti

Salad greens and dressing

4 slices wheatberry bread

Large, heavy frying pan with a lid (10 or 12 inch)

5:30 Dice an onion: Cut off the ends of a whole yellow onion. Cut a checkerboard pattern on top and cut off a slice. Repeat until the onion is all cut up into little cubes.

Put a large heavy frying pan with a lid [   ] on a burner over medium-high heat. Put in the whole pound of meat and the onions, and start to brown by stirring and turning the meat until it is no longer pink.

Sprinkle in about 1/4 teaspoon salt, 1/4 teaspoon pepper, and 2 cloves garlic, chopped in half.

5:50 Now cut up the green pepper. Leave out the central stem and seeds. The pepper can be in small pieces.

Add the pepper to the pan with the meat and keep on cooking.

Add the can of tomato bisque soup.

Fill the can with water and add that, too.

**about
6:00** Now the tricky part. Take out enough spaghetti so that the end of the bunch will cover a circle about as big as a quarter. Break the bunch in half and add it to the liquid in the pan by pressing it down with a spatula. Give it all a big stir, put the cover on, and turn the heat down to medium-low. Stir it—so it won't burn.

6:15 Make a green salad (see inside cover pages). Lift the cover off the pan, and give the dish a big stir. Cover and cook some more.

Set the table.

6:30 Make the wheatberry toast, cut into triangles, and put on the table along with the salad. Serve up the dish and...EAT!

Cold milk is excellent with this little meal.

Paul's Fabulous Meatloaf

A luxurious meatloaf with baked potatoes and peas, devised by my son, Paul.

Start to finish: 1 hour 30 minutes

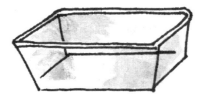

9×5-inch bread pan

Needed:

4 baking potatoes

2 eggs

1½ pounds lean ground round hamburger meat

1 cup bread crumbs, herb-flavored Italian-style

½ teaspoon pureed bottled garlic or ½ teaspoon freshly pressed garlic

Salt

A half stalk celery

1 green pepper

A handful lettuce

1 large yellow onion

⅓ cup catsup (about)

1 slice bacon (if you wish)

Salad greens and dressing

10-ounce package frozen peas

5:00 Turn the oven on to 350°.

Cut the ends off the baking potatoes and put them in the oven right on the rack.

Mix together in a large bowl: 2 eggs, the hamburger meat, the bread crumbs, about 1/2 teaspoon pureed garlic, and about 1/2 teaspoon salt. Be sure the breadcrumbs are thoroughly mixed in.

Then gather a half stalk celery, a green pepper (discard the stem and seeds), a handful of lettuce, and an onion.

Cut the vegetables, even the lettuce, into large pieces—they can be about as big as a quarter.

Add all the vegetables to the mixing bowl with the meat. Just barely mix everything together. Pat it gently into a 9-inch by 5-inch bread pan—don't squish it down!

Shake about 1/3 cup catsup on top of the meatloaf and smear it around with a knife (a little goes a long way).

5:30 Lay a strip of bacon across the top of the meatloaf and put it in the oven. Rest a bit, then...

6:00 Make a green salad with your choice of dressing (see inside cover pages), and keep in the refrigerator 'till dinner time.

6:10 Set the table.

6:20 Cook the frozen peas by following the directions on the package.

6:30 Serve slices of meatloaf and the baked potatoes directly on to dinner plates. If it's too soft, just spoon it out! Put the peas in a serving bowl (if you have one with a lid they will stay hotter), and put the peas and the salad on the table, and ...EAT!

Mom's Plain Old Meatloaf

That's it! Simple and tasty!

Start to finish: 1 hour 15 minutes

Needed:

1 pound lean ground round hamburger meat

1 egg

Salt

Pepper

1 cup bread crumbs or cracker crumbs

Parsley

1 or 2 cloves freshly pressed garlic or ¼ teaspoon pureed bottled garlic

1 onion

1 green pepper

Catsup and a strip of bacon —for a richer meatloaf

4 baking potatoes

14½-ounce can stewed tomatoes

8- or 9-inch pie pan

Don't forget!!

Raw vegetables for salad: celery, carrots, mush-rooms, etc.

Whole wheat toast

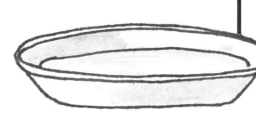

5:15 Turn the oven on to 400°.

5:20 Mix together in a large bowl the meat, an egg, about 1/2 teaspoon salt and a dash of pepper, and 1 cup bread crumbs or cracker crumbs.

Then cut up and add: 1/4 cup parsley, the garlic, onion, and green pepper.

Pat gently into an 8-inch or 9-inch pie pan. If you like, put some catsup (about a half cup) on top and a strip of bacon. Put it in the oven.

5:30 Scrub the baking potatoes, cut off the ends, and put them in the oven right on the rack.

6:15 Open a can of stewed tomatoes and heat on low in a small sauce pan for 10 minutes.

6:20 Cut up celery, carrots, or whatever raw fresh vegetables you have for a salad. Make whole wheat toast.

Put the plate of toast and the salad on the table. Serve each one some meatloaf, baked potato, and tomatoes, and...

6:30 EAT!

P.S. You may want to use small bowls for the tomatoes.

Judith's Meatball Super-supper

A soupy meatball supper with fresh veggies—very satisfying.

Start to finish: 55 minutes

Needed:

1 pound ground chuck hamburger meat

1 teaspoon Worcestershire sauce

1 egg

About ½ package Knorr's dry mushroom soup mix

1 or 2 tablespoons butter

1 cup canned clear chicken broth

4 medium-size red potatoes

2 carrots

2 zucchini squash

1 box cherry tomatoes or 2 large tomatoes

Bread or toast

10-inch heavy frying pan with a lid

5:35 Mix together the meat, Worcestershire sauce, egg, and dry mushroom soup in a large bowl.

Roll into meatballs the size of Ping-Pong balls—about 12—and set aside.

Put 1 tablespoon butter in a large, 10-inch, heavy frying pan with a lid [   ]. Turn the heat to medium-high and lightly brown the meatballs on all sides, turning them with a wooden spoon. Add more butter if needed.

5:50 When they are browned, add 1/2 cup chicken broth and cover the pan. Turn heat down to medium.

Wash the potatoes, cut into thin slices, and add to the pan.

Wash, peel, and cut the carrots into thin slices. Add them to the pan and cover again.

6:05 Pour 1/2 cup more chicken broth into the pan.

Wash—but don't peel—the zucchini and slice them about as thick as your finger. Add to the pan. Put that cover on one more time! Cook until serving time—about 15 minutes or more—over medium-low heat.

Add a bit of water if the pan is too dry.

6:25 Set the table. Wash some cherry tomatoes or cut up large tomatoes and put in a dish on the table. Put some fresh bread or warm toast on the table, too.

6:30 Serve the meatballs and vegetables with some of the hot broth onto dinner plates right at the stove, take to the table, and...EAT!

"Some" Barbeque

Baked short rib beef barbeque—tasty as can be but not terribly spicy.

In the South one always has some barbeque (not just barbeque) with the accent on the some.

Start to finish: 1 hour 30 minutes

Needed:

2 pounds beef short ribs

⅓ cup barbeque sauce, Woody's or your favorite

⅔ cup catsup

4 medium-size russet (baking) potatoes

1 head cabbage

½ cup mayonnaise

1 8½-ounce can pineapple chunks

Any size cookie sheet with sides

5:00   Turn the oven on to 325°.

Scrub, then cut the ends off the baking potatoes and put in the oven right on the rack.

Put the ribs on a cookie sheet with sides.

Mix together the barbeque sauce and catsup and pour it all over the ribs.

5:10   Do not cover in any way and put them in the oven.

6:00   Now make cole slaw:

Use a long knife to cut the cabbage in half.

Put the flat side down on a cutting board and cut about two-thirds of the cabbage into narrow strips about as wide as your finger.

Plop these strips into a big salad bowl and add 1/2 cup mayonnaise.

Then drain the can of pineapple chunks and mix with the mayonnaise and cabbage. Put it in the refrigerator to cool.

6:30   Use oven mitts to take the cookie sheet out of the oven. Take out the potatoes too. Put the cole slaw on the table. Serve the ribs and potatoes on to dinner plates with tongs or a big fork and...EAT!

P.S. For a nice touch, split the tops of the potatoes open with a knife and put a dab of butter in the center.

Chris's Shepherd's Pie

Ground meat and mashed potato casserole—a family favorite.

Start to finish: 1 hour

Needed:

1 pound lean ground round hamburger meat

1 large yellow onion

Salt

Pepper

Instant mashed potatoes for 8

Raw vegetables for salad:

Yogurt dressing (if you wish)

Veggie sauce (inside cover pages)

10-inch oven-proof frying pan

2 quart sauce pan

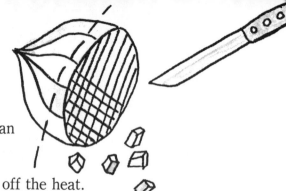

5:30   Turn the oven on to 325°.

5:35   Chop the onion and mix it with the hamburger meat in a big frying pan
[   ].

5:40   Lightly fry it until the meat is all brown—no pink showing, then turn off the heat.

5:55   In the sauce pan [   ], make mashed potatoes for 8 by following the
directions on the package.

6:00   Spoon the mashed potatoes on top of the meat in the 10-inch oven-proof frying pan
and spread them out to make an even layer. Sprinkle the top with about 1/4–1/2
teaspoon salt and pepper and put it in the oven uncovered.

6:10   Make a big plate full of cut up raw vegetables for a salad: celery, tomatoes, turnips, etc.
(whatever you have). The tangy yogurt dressing (see inside cover pages) is a good
addition to this meal.

6:30   EAT!

To make a fancy Shepherd's Pie: add relishes, pickle, mustard, horseradish, etc.
to flavor the meat...or use left over meatloaf for the meat.

Bubala's Chuck Roast

This is a pot roast with gravy and can be built in three minutes.

Start to finish: 2 hours 30 minutes

Garlic Bread

- Turn the oven on to 400°. If you are already cooking something at 375° or more, it will still be OK.
- Cut the French bread in half.
- Put the flat ends down on the cutting board and cut again lengthwise.
- Smash 1 cube of soft margarine or butter in a bowl with a short spatula.
- Squeeze 2 to 4 cloves in a garlic press and mix the garlic puree with the butter. Your family will soon let you know how much garlic and butter to use.
- Butter the bread generously.
- Put in the oven, right on the rack, garlic side up, for 10 minutes.
- Arrange the baked bread in a basket with a napkin over it...and stand back!

Needed:

4-pound piece of beef chuck with the bone, about 2 inches thick

1 2½-ounce package Knorr's dry leek soup mix is best, but all varieties are O.K.

1 15-ounce can Hain's chicken and vegetable soup*

Garlic Bread:
  1 loaf French bread
  ¼ cup butter (½ stick)
  ½ teaspoon freshly pressed garlic

1 box cherry tomatoes

Large, heavy, deep-sided oven-proof pot with a lid

*Hain's is best, but any 14 or 15 ounce vegetable soup will do.

4:00   Turn the oven on to 350°.

Put the chuck roast into a large heavy deep-sided oven-proof pot with a lid
[   ].

Pour the dry leek soup mix on top of the meat.

Open the can of soup and pour the contents over the meat—do not dilute with water.

Put the lid on the pot and put it in the oven.

4:40   Turn the oven down to 300°.

6:00   Set the table.

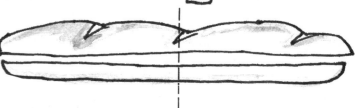

6:10   Make garlic bread (see page 56). Open the oven, and with oven mitts on both hands
lift the pot out and put it on top of the stove. Keep the cover on so it will stay
warm while the garlic bread bakes. Turn the oven up to 400°.

6:20   Put the garlic bread in the oven.

6:25   Wash the tomatoes an put them on the table in a pretty dish. Get help cutting the
meat and serve on to deep dinner plates right at the stove.

6:30   Take the garlic bread out and serve it nice and hot, and…EAT!

Linda's Lasagne

This can be put together and baked immediately. GOOD. No need to boil the noodles first.

This can be assembled an hour before it is baked, but it is even tastier if refrigerated overnight and baked the next day.

Start to finish: 2 hours 30 minutes

Needed:

1 pound lean ground round hamburger meat

Salt, pepper

¾ teaspoon freshly pressed garlic

15½-ounce jar Ragu spaghetti sauce with mushrooms

8-ounce package lasagne noodles (15 to 16 noodles —not "extra wide" type)

16 ounces ricotta cheese

1 egg

About 12 pitted black olives

12 ounces mozzarella cheese

1 cup water

1 cup red wine

1 head romaine lettuce and your favorite salad dressing

9×13-inch cake pan

4:00   Put the meat and the 3/4 teaspoon of garlic (freshly pressed or pureed bottled) into a large heavy frying pan [   ] and cook, stirring, over medium-high heat until it is no longer pink.

4:10   Sprinkle 1/2 teaspoon salt and 1/2 teaspoon pepper over the meat.

Add the jar of Ragu sauce and stir it until it is all blended into the meat.

4:20   Turn off the heat under the frying pan. Now start to build the lasagne.

Put 4 *uncooked* lasagne noodles across the bottom of the 9 × 13-inch cake pan.

Scoop out the ricotta into a small bowl, break an egg into it, and stir them together.

Put half the ricotta cheese mixture over the noodles.

Spread about half the meat sauce mixture over the ricotta cheese.

Now put 6 whole olives or so around the edges.

Next, cut the mozzarella into slices about as thick as your finger and put half of them on top of the meat sauce and ricotta.

Repeat the whole process: make a layer of noodles, then the rest of the ricotta mixture, then the meat sauce, then the rest of the olives, then the mozzarella.

Put on one more layer of noodles. Pour the water and the wine into the dish. The liquid should just cover the top of the noodles—squish the top noodles down into the liquid if necessary.

Last, sprinkle a generous layer of Parmesan cheese all over the top.

Wait until 5:30 to put it in the oven.

5:15   Turn the oven on to 375°.

5:30   Put the lasagne in the oven.

6:00   Start to make garlic bread (see page 56).

6:15   Put the garlic bread in the oven and make a romaine salad (see inside cover pages).

6:25   Take out the lasagne, and cut and serve with a large spatula on to dinner plates. Take out the garlic bread, put it in a basket, cover with a napkin, and put it on the table along with the salad. That's it! EAT!

Fish

Sabina's Summer Soup

A cold, satisfying summer soup: with a good white wine it borders on elegant. Make this in hot weather and refrigerate. It gets better as time goes on. Make the night before for best results.

Start to finish: 10 minutes

Needed:

2 quarts buttermilk

2 4½-ounce cans shrimp ("broken" is cheaper)

2 bunches green onions

2 cucumbers

1 loaf fresh bread or breadsticks

- Pour the buttermilk into a large mixing bowl.

- Open the cans of shrimp, drain the liquid into the sink (do *not* rinse with water), and dump the shrimp into the buttermilk.

- Wash the green onions, cut into small slices, and put them into the buttermilk.

- Wash the cucumbers. Cut them into slices or chunks and put them in, too. You can take the skin off with a vegetable peeler if you wish.

- Cover the bowl and put in the refrigerator for 6 to 8 hours or overnight—that's the best, actually.

- To serve the soup: Pour into small bowls and grind a little fresh pepper on top. Put fresh bread or breadsticks on the table, and...EAT!

What-a-tomato Salad!

*Tomatoes stuffed with a tuna salad—
you can eat in half an hour.
A good hot weather lunch or supper.*

Start to finish: 30 minutes

Needed:

24-ounce can tuna

Salt

Pepper

1 cup mayonnaise

3 stalks celery

½ cup sweet bread
 and butter pickles

4 large ripe tomatoes

4 large lettuce leaves

Breadsticks, fresh bread,
 crackers, whatever you
 have

6:00 Open the can of tuna and push down hard on the lid. Take the can to the sink and drain the liquid out. Put the tuna in a large mixing bowl and add 1 cup of mayonnaise.

Sprinkle on a pinch of salt and a pinch of pepper. Cut 3 stalks celery into pieces about as wide as your finger (1/2 inch), and add to the bowl.

Cut the sweet pickles into smaller pieces and add them to the bowl, too. Give the entire mixture a stir with a big spoon and put it in the refrigerator to cool.

6:15 Now prepare the tomatoes: Wash them, then cut an "X" on top of each one and cut straight down almost to the bottom. Don't cut all the way through. The tomato will open and make a cup for the tuna.

6:25 Wash the lettuce leaves, shake them dry, and place one leaf on each plate.

Put a tomato cup on each leaf and spoon about 1 cup of the tuna mixture into each one.

6:30 Place the breadsticks or bread on the table and serve the salad with iced tea. EAT!

Fish-in-a-packet with Parsley & Butter

Fish baked in the oven with butter, parsley, and garlic—and baked potatoes.

Start to finish: 2 hours

As an alternative to the parsley-butter-garlic mixture, try a small amount (2–3 tablespoons) of red or green salsa. Or use your favorite salad dressing. Bernstein's Creamy Italian dressing gives a hint of tartar sauce to the fish.

Needed:

¼ cup butter (½ stick)

8 romaine lettuce leaves and your favorite salad dressing

4 baking potatoes (russets)

2 cloves garlic or about 1 teaspoon pureed bottled garlic

Several sprigs parsley

4 large fillets fish: sole, halibut, flounder, etc.

1 to 2 tablespoons vegetable oil

1 lemon

French bread

Aluminum foil

4:30   Turn the oven on to 350°.

Scrub the potatoes. Cut the ends off, and put the potatoes in the oven right on the rack.

5:45   Take the butter out of the refrigerator and let it soften.

Wash the lettuce leaves and put on a paper towel to dry.

Smash 2 cloves of garlic in a garlic press (or, second best, spread 1 teaspoon pureed bottled garlic) and mix with the half-stick of butter in a small bowl.

Tear off 4 pieces of foil about 12 inches square and put a few sprigs of parsley in the center of each one.

Lay a piece of fish on top of the parsley and daub a bit of garlic butter on each piece. Gather the edges of foil together to make a packet for each piece of fish.

6:15   Put the fish packets in the oven (among the potatoes).

6:30   Using oven mitts, take the fish packets out of the oven. Open the packets and serve the fish onto plates. Pour the buttery juices left in the packets onto the fish.

Again using mitts, take out the potatoes and place them on the plates. Take everything to the table, including the lemon, cut into wedges, the bread, the salad, and the dressing.

Now, EAT!

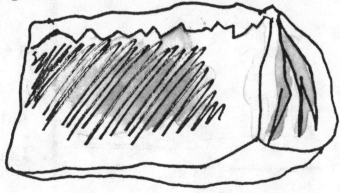

Stanley Eichelbaum's* Good Baked Fish

Instead of the garlic, onion, thyme, etc. mixture that goes over the fish pieces, you can substitute red or green salsa (the Mexican sauce usually near the catsup at the grocery store) or your favorite salad dressing. Use about 3 tablespoons, no more.

Start to finish: 1 hour 30 minutes

*of Cafe Majestic, San Francisco, California

Needed:

4 fish fillets (5–6 ounces each)

1 clove freshly pressed garlic or approximately 1 teaspoon pureed bottled garlic

1 tablespoon chopped onion

½ teaspoon thyme

Pinch oregano

2 tablespoons olive oil

1 tablespoon wine vinegar

4 baking potatoes (russets)

French bread and butter

Salad stuffs

Large, cast-iron frying pan

or

Large, shallow baking dish

5:00 Turn the oven on to 350°.

Scrub and cut the ends off potatoes; then place them right on the oven rack.

Blend together in a small bowl:

1 clove freshly pressed garlic (or approximately 1 teaspoon pureed bottled garlic)
1 tablespoon chopped onion
1/2 teaspoon thyme
pinch oregano
2 tablespoons olive oil
1 tablespoon wine vinegar

Place one tablespoon of this mixture on the fish pieces in the [   ] pan and set aside.

6:00 Make the salad of your choice and turn on the oven to 450°.

6:10 Set table. Make or get out the salad dressing you like best.

6:20 Put the fish pan in the oven *uncovered*.

6:30 Set out French bread, butter, potatoes, salad. Dish up the fish with a spatula...and EAT!

Golden Fried Fish & Buttered Spinach

*People who "never eat fish"
eat this with smiles all over their faces.*

Start to finish: 1 hour 30 minutes

Experienced cooks <u>only</u>!

*This breading method works really well for other foods, too,
such as chicken breasts, veal, pork, etc.
The flour makes the egg stick
and the egg makes the
breadcrumbs stick.*

Needed:

1 loaf fresh, good quality, sliced white bread

About ¾ cup flour

2 eggs

1½ pounds fish fillets, such as sole or flounder

2 bunches spinach

6 to 7 tablespoons butter

1 lemon

Salt

Pepper

Blender

3 shallow bowls

Large stew pot

Large, heavy 12- or 14-inch frying pan

5:00 Stack half of the bread slices, except for the ends, on the cutting board and cut off the crusts. Then cut the stack into quarters. Do the same for the other half of the bread.

Use a blender or food processor to make breadcrumbs: Fill half the blender with squares and process about 20 or 30 seconds until the breadcrumbs are fine and even. Put the crumbs in a shallow bowl or dish and repeat with the rest of the bread.

In another shallow dish put the flour and season it with a little salt and pepper.

Break the eggs into another dish and beat with a fork until smooth.

Now dip a fillet into the flour, first one side and then the other, and shake off any excess. Then dip it into the egg—same thing, lightly on both sides—then let any excess run off. Then lay it in the breadcrumbs and press the breadcrumbs onto the fish so it is well coated. Put the breaded fillet on a cookie sheet or platter. Do this with all of the fish and put the platter in the refrigerator for 20 or 30 minutes to let the breading "dry."

Put any extra breadcrumbs in a plastic bag and freeze for another dinner.

6:00 Cut the bottom stems off the bunches of spinach, discard any really old or torn-up leaves, and wash well in a sinkful of cold water. Drain the spinach in a drainer.

6:10 Melt half the butter in a large stew pot [   ] over medium heat.

Add enough spinach to cover the whole bottom and cook it until it wilts, then add another few handfuls of leaves and stir around. When it wilts add more until all the spinach is in the pot. Sprinkle with a little salt and pepper and a squeeze of lemon juice. Add a little more butter as needed. Stir again and turn the heat down low to keep it warm while you cook the fish.

6:20 In a large frying pan [   ], melt the rest of the butter over medium-high heat. Add the fish fillets and cook in a single layer about 4 to 5 minutes on each side until the breadcrumbs are golden brown.

6:30 Serve the crispy fish very hot with the tender spinach and a wedge of lemon and ...EAT!

breadcrumbs

flour

eggs

Lamb, Ham, Pork & Sausages

Baked Lamb Chops

Very popular, very hearty, very easy. Lamb chops baked in an open pan with cheesy topping.

Start to finish: 2 hours

Needed:

4 large baking potatoes

4 loin lamb chops, ¾" thick or more

6 green onions

1 teaspoon pureed bottled garlic or 3 or 4 cloves freshly pressed garlic to make up about 1 teaspoon garlic

½ cup whipping cream

2 tablespoons grated Parmesan cheese

Stouffer's spinach souffle for 4

Raw vegetables for salad: carrots, celery, peppers, tomatoes, etc.

10-inch heavy frying pan

4:30 Turn the oven on to 350°.

4:35 Scrub the baking potatoes, cut the ends off, and put in the oven right on the rack.

4:45 Put the lamb chops into a large, heavy, oven-proof frying pan or low-sided pyrex dish
[   ].

Cut up the green onions and put them on top of the chops.

Dab about 1/4 teaspoon garlic puree on each chop. Pour the whipping cream over
all and sprinkle 2 tablespoons Parmesan cheese on top.

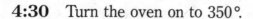

5:00 Put the pan with the chops in the oven.

5:30 Take the cover off the souffle and put it in the oven on the middle rack.

6:20 Set the table.

6:25 Cut up some raw vegetables for a salad and put them on a plate.

6:30 Serve plates with chops, sauce, and potatoes. Put the souffle on the table, and...EAT!

Plain Old Scalloped Potatoes & Ham Casserole

So good and so overlooked.
Potato and ham slices with milk, butter and melted cheese.
Everybody still loves this classic.

Start to finish: 2 hours 30 minutes

Needed:

6 small red or white potatoes

¾ pound pre-cooked ham from the butcher or canned ham

4 tablespoons butter (¼ stick)

3 cups milk

2 to 4 ounces shredded cheddar cheese

2 or 3 stalks celery

1 jar applesauce

Salt

Pepper

8-, 9-, or 10-inch oven-proof casserole

This is one of those slow chop-chop affairs where you get all your ingredients ready and then put the dish together.

4:00   Turn the oven on to 325°.

Wash, then cut the potatoes into slices as thin as a quarter, or as thin as you can, and make a pile of them on the counter.

Cut the ham into small squares and make another pile. You should have about 2 cups ham pieces.

Cut the butter into 3 or 4 slices.

Now put the casserole together. Use an 8-inch, 9-inch, or 10-inch oven-proof casserole dish [   ].

Make a layer of potatoes in the bottom of the dish, using about 1/3 of the pile of potatoes.

Next, put a layer of ham squares, using about half of the ham.

Then put a slice of butter on top of the ham layer.

Make another layer of potatoes.

Make another layer of ham. Add another slice of butter.

Finish with a last layer of potatoes and a slice of butter.

Shake about 1/4 teaspoon salt and 1/4 teaspoon pepper over the top.

Pour over 3 cups milk, then sprinkle shredded cheddar cheese all over the top.

4:30
to
4:45   Put the casserole in the oven uncovered.

6:25   Set the table. Cut up the celery into sticks and put on the table. Put the applesauce in a pretty bowl and set on the table.

6:30   Dinner time!

Jill's Favorite Pork & Rice Dish

A baked casserole, tomatoey pork and rice together —nice and moist. Our illustrator hates tomatoes, yet loves this dish.

Start to finish: 1 hour 45 minutes

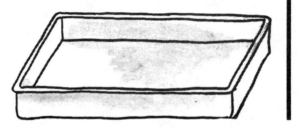

Needed:

Half of a 2½-ounce package Knorr's dry leek soup mix*

1 cup white rice

4 slices pork steak or shoulder, sliced about ½ inch thick, about 1 to 1½ pounds in all

½ teaspoon pureed bottled garlic, or freshly pressed garlic to make ½ teaspoon

10¾-ounce can Campbell's chicken gumbo soup

Salt

Pepper

12-ounce can V-8 juice

Green salad and dressing of your choice

Bread for toasting

9×13-inch cake pan

Knorr's French onion or Lipton's are possible substitutes.

4:45 Turn the oven on to 350°.

Pour the half package soup mix onto the bottom of a 9-inch by 13-inch cake pan
[   ].

Sprinkle the uncooked rice over the soup mix.

Place the pork steaks on top of the rice.

Dot the meat with 4 tiny bits of pureed garlic and sprinkle about 1/4 teaspoon salt and
1/4 teaspoon pepper over everything.

Open the can of soup, spoon it out, and spread over the meat.

Last, pour the V-8 juice over everything.

Cover the pan tightly with foil.

5:00 Put the pan in the oven.

6:00 Make a green salad (see inside cover pages), and put it in the refrigerator to chill.

6:15 Set the table.

6:25 Take the pork dish out of the oven and serve on to dinner plates. Make toast and
place on the side of the plates, put the salad on the table, and...EAT!

Cozy Sausage Supper

Fried sausages and mashed potatoes with a tang!

Start to finish: 1 hour 5 minutes

Needed:

4 tablespoons butter (½ stick)

6 to 8 sausages: bratwurst, bockwurst, hot links, veal, pork, garlic, Polish —you name it

½ bottle or can (6 ounces) ale or beer

Instant mashed potatoes for 8*

12-ounce can creamed corn

If you wish, cottage cheese, applesauce, mustard

Fresh parsley

Celery sticks

10- or 12-inch heavy frying pan

Do not add any salt to this recipe

Mashed potatoes for 8 even though the meal is designed for 4. The mashed potato people estimate skimpily.

5:20 Put 2 blobs of butter (about 2 tablespoons) in a large heavy frying pan
[   ]. Put on the stove over medium heat.

Add the sausages right away and start to cook them, turning every so often with
a fork.

5:30 Add half a can of beer or ale to the sausages—put the rest of the can of beer back in
the refrigerator for Dad or Mom to have with dinner. Then add about ¾ cup of water
to the pan and turn the heat to low. Do *not* cover the pan.

5:50 Turn the oven to "warm," and put in a large ceramic serving platter just to warm it—
don't use plastic. Turn the sausages and make sure there is still a little liquid in the
pan. If not, add about 1/4 cup water and swirl around.

Make instant mashed potatoes for 8 by following the directions on the package.
Be careful not to let the milk-water mixture boil over.

6:05 Turn off the sausages. They will probably be very dark brown, which is fine. Take the
warm platter out of the oven and spoon the mashed potatoes on to it. Make a deep
trench in the middle with the spoon.

Put the sausages in the trench, pour a little liquid from the pan on to the sausages,
and put the whole thing back in the oven.

6:10 Open the can of creamed corn and empty into a small saucepan. Put on a burner over
very low heat, and stir.

6:15 Set the table. Stir the corn. Put some cottage cheese, applesauce, and celery sticks
on a big dinner plate and put it on the table. Check that corn now!

If you like, put a jar of mustard on the table, too.

6:25 Now take the sausage platter from the oven and put sprigs of parsley around the
edges of the plate. Dot the potatoes with the rest of the butter and place the platter
on the table. Serve the creamed corn in a serving bowl and…EAT! Well done!

Company Dinner:

Sahag's Roast Lamb

Swati's Yogurt Dessert

*Roast lamb with vegetables—
a show-off company dinner with a
Middle Eastern flavor.
For 6 to 8 people.*

> Any good cut of beef roast can be
> used with equal success—and only
> one or two humble vegetables will
> do very nicely.

*This is one meal that
your parents can and should help you with—
opening the wine and just hanging around during the
basting (pouring liquid over the meat to keep it moist while it roasts).
You can make the dessert while the meat roasts, but get a
little help with the double boiler for the yogurt.
It should chill a half an hour or so.*

Experienced cooks <u>only</u>!

Start to finish: 2 hours

Needed:

2 or 3 heads garlic

2 medium eggplants or
1 large one

1 red pepper

2 green peppers

3 zucchini squash

3 yellow crookneck squash

3 onions

¾ pound medium size
mushrooms

2 or 3 bay leaves

2 tablespoons olive oil

Leg of lamb with bone,
weighing about 5 to 6
pounds

1 fifth red wine, such as
Zinfandel or burgundy

Large roasting pan

Double boiler

No schedule is given here. Simply allow half an hour preparation time and an hour and a half roasting time.

Turn the oven on to 400°.

Separate the heads of garlic into cloves—peel and set aside.

Wash the eggplant, peppers, and squashes and cut into large chunks.

Peel the onions and cut into quarters.

Wash the mushrooms and leave whole, then set aside.

Put all of the vegetables in a large roasting pan, add the bay leaves, and pour the olive oil over all.

Season with salt and pepper.

Cut off the excess fat from the leg of lamb. Rub it with olive oil and season with salt and pepper. If you want, chop fresh rosemary and rub it all over the meat.

Cut 2 or 3 garlic cloves into slivers—you should have about 8 or 10 slivers in all. With a small sharp knife pierce the leg of lamb in 8 or 10 places and insert a sliver of garlic in each "pocket" made by your knife.

Set the lamb on top of the vegetables (they become a sort of rack for the meat) and put the pan in the 400° oven. Turn the oven down to 350°.

Every 15 minutes or so pour about 1/4 to 1/3 cup red wine from the bottle over the meat and give the vegetables around the meat a stir.

Cook until the meat is done—about 1-1/2 hours.

Take the meat out and put it on a platter. Cover with foil and let it rest 20 minutes or so.

Let the vegetables cook a little more until the juices in the pan are syrupy.

Serve slices of lamb moistened with a little of the juices which have collected on the platter and the hot vegetables. The vegetables are especially delicious cooked this way!

Experienced cooks only!

SWATI'S YOGURT DELIGHT

In the top of a double boiler mix thoroughly 2 8-ounce cartons of vanilla yogurt with 1/2 of a 14-ounce can of Borden's Sweetened Condensed Milk.

When a few small bubbles form—about 2 minutes—pour into pretty glass dishes. Add slices of mandarin oranges or kiwi fruit.

Chill it in the refrigerator for half an hour or so.

Bertie's Muesli (a Granola-type cereal)

God's own original food.
This is a hearty cereal—it takes time to make,
but from then on it's instant!

Start to finish: Allow about 20 minutes

This is a famous dish originally developed by a Swiss doctor for its nutritional balance. It is wonderful to have on hand for a quick meal or when you have a houseful of relatives or company.
Most folks double this recipe.

Needed:

1¾ cups whole oats—not quick oats

½ cup brown sugar

1⅓ cups milk

¼ cup wheat germ

½ lemon

½ cup raisins

½ cup shelled walnut pieces

2 juicy apples

If you wish add:
Fresh fruit such as plums, grapes, berries, peaches, bananas, etc.

Whipping cream

Big mixing bowl, or perhaps a large roasting pan!

Get out a *big* mixing bowl [   ].

Dump 1-3/4 cups whole oats into the bowl, then add 1/2 cup brown sugar.

Pour in the 1-1/3 cups milk and sprinkle 1/4 cup wheat germ on top.

Cut the lemon in half and squeeze one half over everything.

Toss in 1/2 cup raisins and 1/2 cup walnut pieces.

Wash, then cut the apples in half. Using the largest holes of a grater, shred the apples down to the core directly onto a dinner plate.

Slide the apples and their juice into the bowl and stir the mixture with a big spoon until it is all blended together.

You can eat it right away or cover the bowl and store in the refrigerator. It will keep as long as a week.

You can add fruit and more milk and eat it as a cereal, or add whipping cream and fruit and it becomes a dessert.

The longer you keep it, the more milk you will need to add to it.

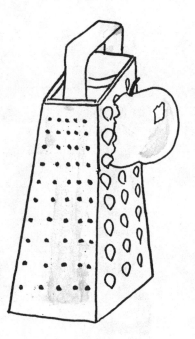

Desserts

Miss Nancy's Chocolate Cake

This recipe comes from "Miss Nancy" Barber, our next-door neighbor for 35 years. She was reared by a superb cook on a Southern plantation.

It's exactly as it was—I only added a little vanilla.

Imagine yourself in the dark old kitchen house quickly beating this simple, one-bowl cake.

It's particularly delicious with a glass of cold milk.

Needed:

2 ounces (2 squares) unsweetened chocolate

1 cup all-purpose flour

½ teaspoon salt

1 cup sugar

1 egg

⅓ cup sour cream

1 teaspoon baking soda

1 teaspoon vanilla

2 to 3 tablespoons confectioner's sugar

8-inch round cake pan

hammer

- Turn the oven on to 350°.

- Grease an 8-inch round cake pan.
  Pour 1/2 cup water into a small saucepan and place on the stove over high heat.

- Put the chocolate squares inside an ordinary clear plastic bag on a magazine on the floor and pound it with a hammer. Give it a lot of good whacks until the chocolate pieces are about as big as a pea.

- Empty the chocolate pieces into a mixing bowl and carefully pour the hot water over them. Stir the chocolate until it is melted smooth, then set aside to cool.

- Measure out 1 cup flour. Gently spoon the flour into a measuring cup and scrape the extra off the top—don't press down. Measure 1/2 teaspoon salt and add to the flour. Set aside.

  When the chocolate mixture is cool enough—stick your finger in it to test, if it is not warm and not cold—proceed.

- Measure 1 cup sugar and add to the chocolate. Stir it around once or twice. Add the flour and salt and stir a little more. Break in the egg and beat it with a fork about 20 times until it looks bubbly.

- Stir in 1/3 cup sour cream, 1 teaspoon soda, and 1 teaspoon vanilla.

- Now comes the beating of the cake. If you are true to tradition, you will beat quickly by hand with a wooden spoon, 100 strokes. It is easier and more fun to do it this way than to dig out an electric beater.

- Pour the batter into the cake pan and bake for about 25 or 30 minutes. It is done when the center springs back to a light touch of your finger tip or when a knife inserted in the center comes out clean. Allow the cake to cool 1 hour or more, then take it out of the pan and put it on a pretty dish. Put 2 tablespoons powdered sugar in a strainer and swirl it around with a spoon right over the cake. This makes a pretty snowflake effect. To be really uptown, put a paper doily over the cake before dusting with sugar and it will make a fancy pattern through the holes.

Taxi-driver Gingerbread

This recipe was pressed into my hand on a grimy slip of paper by a taxi-driver who claimed it was his grandmother's and the best ever. I agree...quick and easy, too.

A one-bowl affair.

Needed:

½ cup butter (1 stick)
—don't substitute
margarine

2¼ cups all-purpose
flour

½ cup sugar

½ teaspoon salt

1 teaspoon ginger

1 teaspoon cinnamon

¼ teaspoon cloves

2 teaspoons baking
soda

1 egg

1 cup molasses,
preferably dark

1 cup boiling water

9×13-inch cake pan

- Turn the oven on to 325°.

- Take a stick of butter out of the refrigerator to soften.

- Measure all of the dry ingredients into a mixing bowl and blend them all together with a pastry blender or whisk.

- Measure 1 cup cold water into a small saucepan and place it on the stove over high heat.

  While it heats to boiling, mix the rest of the ingredients into the batter:

- Make a little hollow place in the center of the flour mixture and break an egg into it. Beat the egg with a fork until little bubbles form—or about 20 strokes.

- Pour in 1 cup molasses.

- If the butter is not soft, put the stick (still wrapped in paper) on the counter and beat with a rolling pin until it is soft. Scrape the butter off the paper and add to the egg and molasses.

- Carefully pour the boiling water into the center and beat everything together. It will look lumpy and discouraging at this point. Beat about 30 strokes *or* until the butter is all smooth.

- Grease a 9-inch by 13-inch cake pan with butter or margarine, pour in the batter, and bake for 35 to 45 minutes. It is done if the center springs back when you press it lightly or if a clean knife inserted in the center comes out clean. Take it out and let it cool.

  It is very good with a shaving of sweet butter on top.

  (Take it in your hand, go climb a tree, walk in the snow...)

Helen's Harvest Bars

This recipe was adapted from a professional, small-town baker who finally gave me his recipe after much begging. It began: "10 pounds eggs, 16 pounds flour," etc. Big help!

Needed:

3 eggs

1 cup sugar

1 cup brown sugar

¾ cup vegetable oil

2 cups flour

1 cup walnuts, coarsely chopped

2 cups raisins

½ teaspoon cinnamon

½ teaspoon salt

10½ × 15½-inch cookie sheet with sides

- Turn the oven on to 350°.
- Break the eggs into a mixing bowl and beat slightly—about 20 strokes.
- Add the sugars and vegetable oil, and mix.
- Then add the flour, walnuts, raisins, cinnamon, and salt. Mix all together.
- Pour onto a 10½ × 15½-inch greased cookie sheet with sides. Spread to an even layer with a wet table knife.
- Bake for 25 minutes or until golden on top. They are better underdone than overdone.
- Remove from the oven, wait 10 minutes, and cut into squares.

These go well with strong black coffee.

Dr. Ashe's "Lefse*"

A Scandanavian potato pancake.

Needed:

1 small package flour tortillas

3 to 4 tablespoons butter

3 to 4 tablespoons your favorite jam (apricot is great)

About 1 teaspoon cinnamon

- Turn the oven on to 350°.
- Wrap 3 or 4 tortillas in foil to make a tight packet and place in the hot oven for about 10 minutes.
- Take the packet out of the oven and butter the tortillas generously.
- Smear a bit of jam in the center of each one. Sprinkle with a little cinnamon, roll them up, and…EAT!

Everyday Cookies (Chocolate Chip)

This is a large recipe for a dry cookie mixture to be made ahead and stored in the refrigerator. It can then be finished with the addition of egg, milk, vanilla, and chocolate chips, nuts, etc., and baked in small batches. Instant cookies! This makes enough for 4 batches.

The only "health cookie" that I've ever eaten that doesn't taste like one.

Needed:

Dry cookie mixture:

2 cups whole-wheat flour

2 cups all-purpose flour

2 teaspoons baking soda

2 teaspoons salt

2 cups sugar

1 cup brown sugar

2 cups shortening or 1 pound soft margarine

3 cups old-fashioned rolled oats

1 cup wheat germ

Big mixing bowl or roasting pan

To make 1 batch cookies: about 2 dozen

3 cups dry cookie mixture (above)

1 egg

¼ cup milk

1 teaspoon vanilla

½ cup chocolate chips, or dates, raisins, walnuts, dried apricots, coconut, peanut butter, etc.

- Mix together the flours, soda, salt, and sugars in a big mixing bowl. Cut the shortening or margarine into chunks and, with your fingers, work it into the flour mixture until it looks like fine crumbs. Stir in the oats and wheat germ and mix thoroughly. Store in the refrigerator in a large container with a tight-fitting lid.

- When you want cookies in a hurry: turn the oven on to 350°. Combine 3 cups dry cookie mixture, 1 egg, 1 teaspoon vanilla, 1/4 cup milk and mix thoroughly. Then stir in 1/2 cup chocolate chips, or dates, nuts, etc. Drop by heaping teaspoons onto the greased sheet and bake 10 to 12 minutes. These are just right... sustaining and not overly sweet. You can eat them, well, every day.

Marion's Yogurt Pie

A winner! I like the brown sugar topping the best. French students eat yogurt with brown sugar, and it appeals to me—so simple and classy. It's somehow glamorous.

Needed:

2 eggs

1 cup (8 ounces) plain Yoplait yogurt or your favorite plain yogurt

⅓ to ½ cup sugar (depending on the sweetness of the yogurt)

8-inch or 9-inch prepared graham cracker pie shell

1 cup fresh or canned berries or fruit for topping, or ¼ cup brown sugar

- Turn the oven on to 350°.

- Break the eggs into a mixing bowl and beat until thoroughly blended. Stir in the yogurt and sugar.

  Pour the mixture into the pie shell and add the topping —fruits, berries, brown sugar—whatever you are using.

- Bake for about 30 minutes until the pie looks "set."

- The middle should still be quite soft when you jiggle it. Remove from the oven and let cool; then chill in the refrigerator until serving time.

Simple Sherbet

A delightful texture, both chunky and smooth at the same time.

Needed:

2 cups crushed pineapple

2 cups buttermilk

Glass bread pan

- Mix the pineapple and buttermilk together and pour into a glass bread pan or plastic container and freeze. When it is slushy and partially frozen (in about 1 hour) stir thoroughly. Re-freeze until firm like ice cream. Remove from the freezer about 10 to 20 minutes before serving time to soften slightly.

"Homemade" Ice Cream

- Store-bought ice cream and cookies. Let the ice cream soften an hour or so. Transfer it to a big bowl. Crumble the cookies and stir them in. Then re-freeze. Try vanilla with Oreo cookies, butter-pecan (or any caramel flavored ice cream) with gingersnaps, etc. This last combination is snappy! Bill Ortman, of Ortman's Ice Cream Parlor—the Ten Speed/Celestial Arts annex— suggests caramel ice cream, as sadly, Butter Brittle, exists no more.

Ruth's Fruit Crisp-in-a-crust

A unique, rich pie with a crumb top.

Needed:

8-inch or 9-inch frozen pie crust (one of Mom's homemade)

Topping:
1 stick butter
¾ cup brown sugar
¾ cup flour

Fruit:

6 to 8 cooking apples, cored and sliced (you can use your apple corer)

or

3 pounds apricots, washed, pitted, and quartered

or

3 pounds plums, peaches, etc., washed, pitted, and sliced

or

4 cups berries, washed, drained, and hulled, if necessary

Super with vanilla ice cream or sweetened whipped cream

8- or 9-inch pie pan

- Turn the oven on to 450°.

- Take out the frozen pie crust, unwrap it, and let it thaw to room temperature.

- Make the topping next: Melt the stick of butter in a small saucepan over medium heat. Let it cool a bit, then add the brown sugar and flour. Stir it together, then set aside.

- Now fill the pie shell with the prepared fruit—apples, berries, whatever you have. Be sure the fruit is pitted and clean but do not add any sugar to it.

- With your fingers place clumps of the topping all over the fruit and place the pie in the oven.

- After 10 minutes, turn the oven down to 350° and bake 40 to 50 minutes more. When it is done, remove it from the oven and let cool at least 30 minutes. Serve warm or well cooled, garnished with vanilla ice cream or sweetened whipped cream.

Sweetened whipped cream:

Put ½ pint whipping cream in a bowl, add a few drops vanilla extract and 1 to 2 tablespoons sugar. Beat until soft peaks begin to form.

Five Pie Crusts

(for Mom to make)

Needed:

Blend together:

4 cups flour

1 tablespoon sugar

2 teaspoons salt

¾ cup Crisco

In a cup mix together:

½ cup water

1 tablespoon vinegar

1 egg

**Stir this into the dry
    mixture**

Form 5 balls of pie dough. Roll out into crusts, fit and pat
    firmly into pie pans, wrap in plastic, and freeze.

Jill Graham's Warm Fruit Compote

Needed:

**1 8½-ounce can
    apricots**

**1 8½-ounce can
    Bing cherries**

**1 8½-ounce can
    peaches**

**1 8½-ounce can
    pears**

3 tablespoons brandy

1 teaspoon cinnamon

**2 tablespoons brown
    sugar**

Sour cream

Shallow baking dish

- Turn the oven on to 275°.

- Open all the cans and spoon out all of the fruit into a
    shallow baking dish [   ].

- Pour about half of the juice from the cherries, apricots,
    and peaches into the baking dish. You will need about
    1 cup of juice.

- Then add the brandy, cinnamon, and brown sugar. Stir
    it a little and put the dish in the oven uncovered.

    Bake about 30 minutes.

    Serve warm with a little sour cream and shortbread
    or butter cookies.

Going-into-the-Apple-crisp-business (Lindsey's Crisp)

The recipe makes enough for 5 or 6 crisps. Store the extra topping in a tighly-closed container in the refrigerator—it will keep well for 5 or 6 weeks. That way you can make a fine dessert on the spur of the moment.

Needed:

Topping, enough for 5 or 6 crisps:

1¾ cups all-purpose flour

¼ cup sugar

1¾ cups brown sugar

1 teaspoon cinnamon

1½ sticks (¾ cup) soft butter

1 cup lightly-toasted chopped nuts (walnuts, almonds, etc.)

Fruit for 1 crisp:

8 to 10 apples, or about 4 cups berries or sliced peaches, apricots, etc.

To make the topping: Combine the flour, sugars, and cinnamon in a large mixing bowl. Cut the soft butter into pieces and add to the bowl. Use two knives or a pastry blender to blend the butter into the mixture until it looks light and crumbly; then add the nuts.

To complete the crisp: Peel*, core, and slice the apples—use an apple slicer if you have one. You should have about 4 cups apples or other fruit. Place the apples in an 8-inch square cake pan [   ], or a 9-inch pie pan[   ]

Sprinkle 1 cup of topping over the fruit and bake at 325° for about 1 hour, or until lightly browned. Remove from the oven and serve warm, or allow to cool. Top with sweetened whipped cream, plain whipping cream, or vanilla ice cream.

To toast nuts:

Spread out chopped nuts on a cookie sheet and place in a 325° oven for 5 minutes.
*Some prefer the bolder flavor of unpeeled apples.

Dessert Dutch Bunny

This makes a wonderful dessert and a really show-off breakfast.

Needed:

4 tablespoons butter

4 large eggs or
5 small ones

1 cup milk

1 cup all-purpose
flour

About 6 tablespoons
jam or jelly or 1 to
2 cups fresh fruit
or berries

2 to 4 tablespoons
powdered sugar

Nutmeg or cinnamon

9×13-inch cake pan

5:45 Turn the oven on to 425°.

Put 4 blobs of butter (about 4 tablespoons) in a 9×13-inch cake pan [   ] and put the pan in the oven.

In a mixing bowl, beat the eggs; then add the milk, then add the flour. It will be a little lumpy —that's OK.

6:00 With an oven mitt, take the cake pan out of the oven and pour in the egg mixture. Return the pan to the oven.

6:30 Use an oven mitt and take the pan out of the oven again.

Spread the jam or jelly in a large circle in the center of the Dutch Bunny or sprinkle the berries or fruit there. Shake on a little powdered sugar, about 2 or 4 tablespoons, and a tiny bit of nutmeg or cinnamon.

Serve onto plates and sit down and PARTAKE!

Marion Cunningham's Chocolate Chip Squares

This is it—none better. My choice of all chocolate chip bars.

Needed:

1½ cups all-purpose
flour

1½ teaspoons baking
powder

½ teaspoon salt

1 cup sugar

⅓ cup vegetable oil

2 eggs, slightly beaten

2 cups (12 ounces)
semisweet choc-
olate morsels

If you wish,
½ cup chopped nuts

8-inch square pan

- Turn the oven on to 350°.

- Grease and flour an 8-inch square pan.

- Stir and toss together the flour, baking powder, salt, and sugar. Add the oil and eggs and beat until thoroughly combined (mixture will be stiff).

- Stir in the chocolate morsels and nuts. Scrape the dough into the prepared pan and use your moistened fingertips to smooth the top and spread it evenly.

Bake for about 30 minutes, or until the top is golden brown and a toothpick inserted into the center comes out clean, or with just a little chocolate on it. Remove from the oven and cool in the pan on a rack, then cut into 2-inch squares. They come out nice and high— a little over an inch.

You can find this recipe in Marion Cunningham's wonderful *Fanny Farmer Baking Book*.

Easy Dessert Ideas

Here are some simple and easy dessert ideas.

Chocolate Graham Crackers

Pour chocolate sauce on top of graham crackers—a good old combination but nice because it's so fresh.

Lillian Gish's* Favorite Dessert

Poach or boil apples in fresh orange juice, puree in a blender, and serve very cold in a *pink* bowl with sweetened whipped cream.

*If you don't know who this person is—ask your Grandma.

Instant Strawberry Shortcake

(an old Girl Scout method)

Top shortbread cookies with sliced, sweetened strawberries and whipped cream.

Instant "Cheesecake"

Slather an oatmeal cookie with about 1/4 inch of cream cheese and top with a dot of jam. Try it with a little chocolate sauce in the center for "chocolate cheesecake."

Fancy Frozen Candy Desserts

These were tested in a particularly wild and heady session with eight students at Cornell School, Albany, California.

Here are the results:
First place winner: The Charleston Chew—fabulous
Second place: Mars Bar
Third Place: Three Musketeers, Whatchamacallit, Snickers, and Milky Way

Chill the candy bars in the freezer. Serve them cut into small bite-size pieces and present with a flourish on a pretty plate.

Chilled Plums

Chill canned purple plums. Serve in small glass bowls with gingersnaps. This is a particularly satisfying ending to a pork or lamb dinner.

Chilled Grapes

Wash a bunch of seedless grapes, any variety; place in an *open* plastic bag, and put in the freezer for an hour or so. These are very tasty following a barbeque dinner.